This hothouse book belongs to

....

This edition published in 2012
Cottage Farm
NN6 0BJ

Text and illustrations © Sally Hunter, 2011

www.humphreys-corner.com

SHE001 1012
2 4 6 8 10 9 7 5 3 1

ISBN: 978-1-78197-132-1

Printed and manufactured in China

Humphrey's Jungle Adventure

Sally Hunter

Humphrey's little friend, George, who lived next door, had come over to play for the afternoon.

Humphrey was excited to show him his new, big, jungle adventure book!

Humphrey fetched his really good lion mask, too.
"Look George, I made him at nursery."

Then George had a really good idea.
"Humphrey! Let's have our very own jungle adventure."

"Back in a minute!"
shouted George.
He disappeared through
the hole in the hedge,
into his garden.

"Hmmm,"
thought Humphrey,
"Mom's plant pots
could be very
useful."

"Look, Humphrey," said George, "I've brought Stripey."

George had his best toy in his arms — a soft, floppy tiger, with a purr in his tummy.

"Good idea, George," said Humphrey.
"I found these for our jungle, too."

Tiger

Next, Humphrey asked
Baby Jack nicely, if he could
please borrow Cheeky Monkey.

"Thank you, Baby Jack,
I will bring him back soon."

Monkey

Then, Humphrey looked for Polly Parrot. Where had she gone?

George helped, too.

"Oh, there you are!" said Humphrey. Polly had been sitting in the treehouse.

Parrot

Humphrey asked Lottie if
Bear was allowed to come
and play jungles, too.

Lottie said, "He was about
to have his tea, but okay then.
Make sure you look
after him well!"

Bear

Humphrey remembered he had taken Sammy Snake for a drive in his little, red car.

"Come on, Sammy. Come and be in our jungle!"

Hurray! We have lots of animals now.

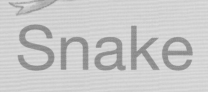

Snake

Suddenly, Humphrey and
George heard a BIG noise!
A loud, growly kind of noise—
G-R-R-R!

A big, furry lion had come
into Humphrey and
George's jungle!

Lion

Phew! It was just a friendly Daddy lion.

Humphrey and George each had a lion ride.

Then they had pineapple juice and chocolate animal biscuits in their tropical jungle.

Can you remember all the animals in Humphrey and George's jungle?

Tiger

Bear

Snake

Monkey

Parrot

Lion

Goodbye,
jungle animals.

Goodbye, George!
See you soon, Humphrey!

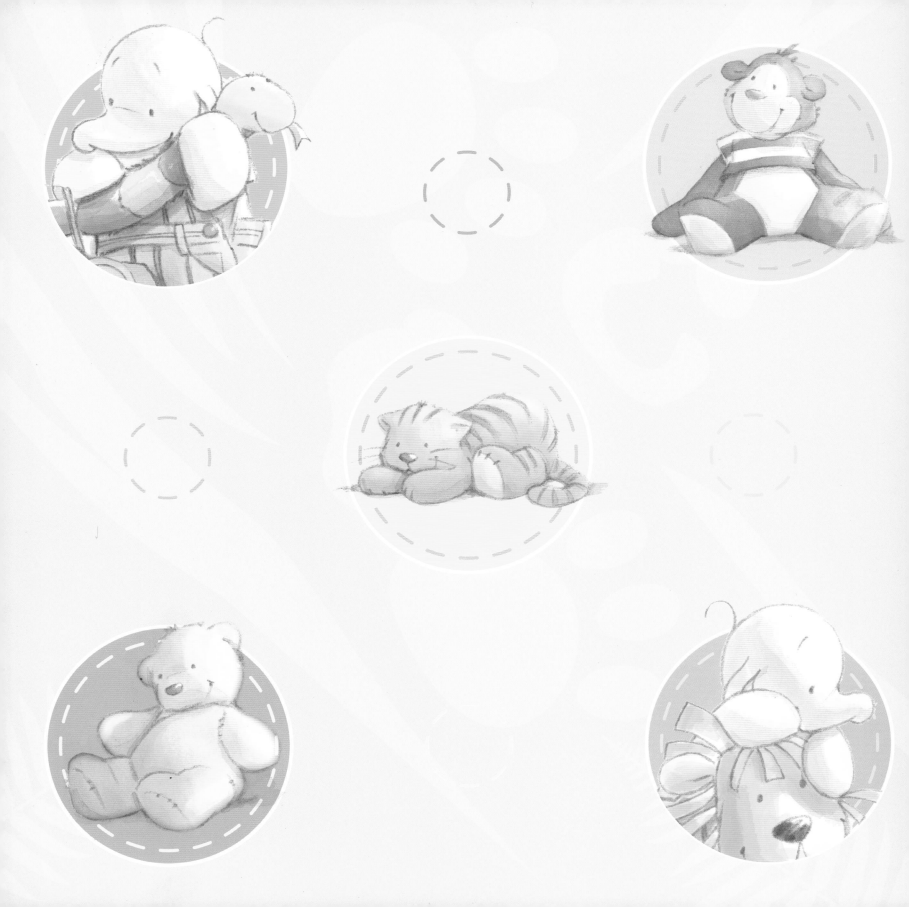